The Phantom of the Opera

The audience screamed in terror.

People jumped from their seats, confused and frightened. There were dead and wounded among them.

Meanwhile, Christine had fainted on the stage. I leaped to where she lay and carried her through a secret passage. I had left a white horse from the stable in the first cellar. I put Christine on his back and I took her down, down, down.

The Phantom of the Opera

by Gaston Leroux
adapted by Kate McMullan
illustrated by Paul Jennis

A STEPPING STONE BOOK™

Random House 🏠 New York

www.steppingstonesbooks.com
www.randomhouse.com/kids

Library of Congress Cataloging-in-Publication Data
McMullan, Kate.
The phantom of the opera / by Gaston Leroux ; adapted by Kate McMullan.
   p.   cm.
"A Stepping Stone book."
SUMMARY: A disfigured musical genius who lives beneath the Paris Opera House
falls in love with a beautiful soprano and, in his desperation to have his love
returned, embarks on some terrifying means toward that end.
ISBN 0-394-83847-5 (pbk.) — ISL √ 0-394-93847-X (lib. bdg.)
[1. Horror stories.] I. Leroux, Gaston, 1868–1927. Fantôme de l'Opéra.
II. Title.   III. Series.
PZ7.M2295   Ph   2001   [Fic]—dc21   2001019103

Chapter 1

I curse the day I was born. When my mother saw me, she screamed in horror!

I was ugly. Worse than ugly. My face was like a skull. My nose was sunk in. It looked as if I had no nose at all. My eyes were small and yellow. My body was a skeleton with skin. But inside, I was a child, not a monster. Not yet.

My mother never kissed me. Never! She could not bear to look at me. I was so horrible that she made me wear a mask. My father never even saw my face.

Did I have a name? I do not remember one. I remember only harsh words from my mother. And the sting of my father's belt. I remember only fear and pain. As soon as I was old enough, I ran away.

I ran from the little town in France where I was born. By day, I hid. By night, I wandered. No one saw my face.

I did not know where I was going. And I did not care.

In the dark, I sang to myself. Unlike my body, my voice was very beautiful. My songs rang out clear and fine in the night air.

Sometimes people heard me sing.

"Where is that lovely voice coming from?" they would ask. "It sounds like an angel!"

"Beautiful singer!" they would call. "Come out! Show us who you are!"

Show them what? The body of a skeleton? A skull with a mask? I stayed hidden in the dark.

When I got hungry, I looked in garbage cans for scraps of food. I picked pockets and learned the ways of the street.

One night I saw tents far off. As I came closer, I saw that it was a fair. Lights shone. People walked from tent to tent, talking and laughing.

I straightened my mask and walked to the fair. A man inside the gate called, "Come one! Come all! This way to the Freak Show! See things you have never seen! See the lady with a beard! See the man with three eyes! Come! This way!"

A lady with a beard? A man with three eyes?

"See the lady with fish scales!" the man called. "See the fattest man in the world!"

I followed the signs to the Freak Show and bought a ticket. I blinked beneath my mask. I could not believe my eyes! There she was—a lady with a beard! Next to her was a man with a funny spot on his forehead. It looked like a third eye!

The lady and the man were like no one I had ever seen before. I walked on. I saw the fattest man in the world. And the lady with fish scales. They were strange and ugly. They were . . . like me!

I spoke to the Fat Man. "I want to stay with the fair," I told him.

"This is no place for a boy," he said. "Go home to your mama."

"I have no home," I said. "And I never had a mother."

I pulled off my mask. The Fat Man stared at me just the way people stared at him.

Then he nodded. "I see," he said. "You *do* belong here."

The Fat Man took me to the manager. The manager looked at my skull face and my bony, white body. He smiled.

"Yes," he said. "Stay with us! I have an idea for you!"

The next night, I did not need a ticket for the Freak Show. I was in it. People paid money to see me.

"Come one! Come all! Right this way!" the man called. "See the most horrible face in the world! See the Living-Dead Boy!"

That was me. The most horrible face in the world. The Living-Dead Boy.

At night, people came to look at me. My little yellow eyes gleamed in the dark. I took off my mask. People

screamed and ran from my tent! But they bought more tickets. They came back to look again. I made money for the fair. And for myself.

For the first time in my life, I felt at peace. I had found others like myself. The Living-Dead Boy was where he belonged.

Chapter 2

During the day, the show was closed. I talked with the other freaks. I ate with them. But I always wore my mask.

"What is your name?" the Fortune Teller asked me one day.

"I have no name," I told her.

"You must have a name," she said kindly. "Come. We will find out what it is."

She sat down at a table opposite me. She waved her hands over a crystal ball. "Your name is here," she said. "It is Erik."

Erik. I liked the sound of it. I liked having a name. And even better, I liked having a friend.

The Fortune Teller taught me more than my name. She taught me how to do tricks with cards and coins. Soon I was better than she was.

The Fortune Teller's husband was an escape artist called the Rubber Man. He could tie his arms and legs into knots. He could curl into a tiny ball. In his act, a man tied him with ropes. Another man locked him in chains. But the Rubber Man always escaped. He showed me how to do it too.

I was not unhappy. No. By day, I learned tricks. I wanted to learn everything! I learned more than any boy in school. By night, I scared people. I began to like my power to frighten.

Yet at times I was lonely. The Fortune Teller loved the Rubber Man. And he loved her. But no one loved Erik. No one.

At those times I would go off alone and sing to myself. My beautiful voice gave me peace.

One day a man from a bigger fair promised me more money. So I went with him.

At the new fair I had a new name. Erik, the Living Skeleton! People paid high prices to see my skull face.

And I had a new friend—the Magician. He taught me how to make things disappear. And how to bring them back again. I helped him build his trapdoors.

My favorite act at the new fair was

Madam Delia and her Talking Doll. Madam Delia wore a hat with purple feathers. She held a big doll on her lap. When she spoke to it, the doll answered. It could really talk!

"Madam Delia," I said to her one day. "How do you make your doll talk?"

"What a thing to ask, Erik!" she said. "I never tell my secrets to anyone."

But I kept asking and asking. At last Madam Delia gave in. She showed me how she used her own voice to make the doll talk. She taught me how to throw my voice too. Such fun! Soon my voice could go anywhere. Dogs seemed to sing! Men seemed to bark!

Before long, I was better than Madam Delia. How Madam Delia wished she had not shown me her magic! She whispered against me. She told the other fair people that I would steal their tricks. She was right.

Soon I had no friends. I felt confused. Was learning the same as stealing? Then I would steal! In the dark of night, I left that fair. There were other fairs. I could always get a job.

I traveled from fair to fair, stealing

tricks from everyone I met. I was not just Erik, the Living Skeleton. I had a magic act. I made things disappear. I made women sing in donkey voices. I was an escape artist, too. No longer a shy boy, I felt sure of myself.

I grew famous in my way. The star of the Freak Show. A fair would have a big sign for me. People from far-away lands stopped at the fairs. Their eyes grew wide at what they saw me do. And so my fame spread across the world.

One night a man called the Persian spoke to me after the show.

"We have heard of you in faraway Persia," he said. "The Shah has sent me to find you. He invites you to stay in his palace. You will live like a king!"

Me, Erik, live like a king? Why not?

Chapter 3

The Shah of Persia could be cruel, but he was kind to me. He liked my magic.

"I can do more than these tricks," I told him one day. "Let me plan a palace for you!"

"What kind of palace?" asked the Shah.

"A magic palace!" I said. "With secret passages and trapdoors! You could come and go unseen. You could hear all that is said in the palace. You could spy into any room!"

The Shah laughed with delight. He put me in charge of his best workers.

During the many months it took to build the new palace, I lived like a king. It was just as the Persian had promised. No longer was I Erik, the freak. I was Erik the builder. And the Shah was my friend. Or so I thought.

At last the magic palace was done. The Shah loved it! As a surprise, I added a torture chamber to amuse him. Only the Shah and I knew the dark secrets of the palace.

One night I was roaming through a hidden passage. I heard the Shah talking to his special guard in the throne room.

"Put his yellow eyes out," the Shah said. "Then he will never build another magic palace. No other king will have what I have!"

My heart jumped! Had I heard

right? Did the Shah want to blind me?

"No," the Shah went on. "That is not enough. Erik is too clever. Even blind, he could plan another palace. He must be killed!"

"As you wish," the guard said.

Tears filled my eyes. My heart was breaking! I had thought I had a friend. But I was wrong. I had only another enemy.

As I stumbled away, I bumped into the Persian.

"Hurry!" he whispered. "I brought you here. Now I will help you run for your life!"

The Rubber Man's lessons were useful. I curled into a tiny ball. I squeezed into a wooden box with a sliding lid. The Persian put the box on a train bound for Turkey.

The Persian stayed behind. Later, I learned what had happened.

"Where is Erik?" the Shah demanded.

"I do not know," the Persian said.

"I will put out *your* eyes if you do

not find him!" cried the Shah.

The Persian took a walk by the sea to think. On the beach, he saw a corpse washed up by the waves. Birds had eaten its eyes out and had pecked away much of its skin. The Persian dressed the body in my clothes and brought it to the Shah.

"Here is Erik," the Persian said.

"Good!" said the Shah. "Now the

secrets of my palace are safe!"

But how wrong he was! In Turkey, I slid out of the box. I presented myself to the Sultan. He became my new friend.

I planned an even better palace for him with a more terrible torture chamber. And for him, I made robots. I dressed them just like the Sultan. They could walk and they could

speak in his voice. People were fooled. They thought they were talking to the Sultan. But the Sultan was really home in bed!

"These robots are grand!" the Sultan told me one night. "And they are all mine. No one else has such robots, Erik. No one!"

His words made me remember other words. The Shah's words. How long would it be before the Sultan would want me dead?

Chapter 4

Once more, I ran. Yet I was tired of running, tired of Shahs and Sultans. All I wanted to do was live like other people.

I traveled back to France and worked as a builder of ordinary houses.

Then all Paris began to buzz with excitement. A new opera house was to be built in the heart of the city. I was given the contract to build the foundation.

What an opera house it was going

to be! Huge. Made of the finest marble. Yet the beauty of the Opera House did not interest me. My work was what lay below the Opera House.

There were five cellars going deep into the earth. Stables for the horses used in the operas. Fourteen furnaces. Dressing rooms for over five hundred singers and dancers. One hundred closets for musical instruments. At the bottom of the fifth cellar was a lake. Its water could be pumped up to the stage to make waterfalls. It was all a perfect playground for me!

One day, I was working in the first cellar. I glanced up and saw the Persian.

I greeted him warmly. "What are you doing in Paris?"

"Looking for you," he said.

For a moment I was pleased.

"I saved your life," he continued. "That makes me responsible for you." The Persian sighed. "I know what dangerous things you can do. I must keep an eye on you."

"Spy on me?" I cried. "No! My life is my own!"

The Persian shook his head and walked away.

I would show him! He would never know what Erik was up to. Never!

So it was that I began to work after hours. For years after the Opera House was completed, I continued working. Below the Paris Opera House was a whole world! My world! I built secret passages and trapdoors, false walls and trick mirrors in the dressing rooms.

I built a house for myself by the

lake. My bedroom was large, with black walls and the best organ ever made. There was another bedroom and a dining room. Outside, walls of rock hid my cozy little house. No one could see it was there. Like me, my house wore a mask.

I added a special touch to my house. A torture chamber to make the most wicked Shah or Sultan sigh with envy. At first, it looked like a harmless forest. But it was a forest with only one tree. An iron tree. Mirrors turned that tree into a forest. Lights could make it a forest of death!

Under the floor, I stored gunpowder. Enough to blow a big hole in Paris! It made me feel powerful to know I had it. Maybe I would never use it. But maybe I would!

Chapter 5

At first, I liked living under the Opera. I had made a kingdom for myself in the dark.

I spent weeks at a time sitting at my organ, writing music. And then there was always some little improvement to add to the cellars. A new trapdoor, maybe, or a two-way mirror.

Yet as the years passed, the longing to live like others grew.

One day when I was out shopping, I bought a mask with a false nose. And—a fine suit of opera clothes!

That night, I tried on my new face. I looked different, but not too frightening. I put on my new clothes and bought a ticket for the opera. So what if I still looked like a skeleton? I was doing what other people did.

Oh, how I loved the opera! The music seemed to take away my pain.

I began going to the opera each night. The little ballet girls scurried away from me in the halls. Men and women drew back as I passed. Soon people began telling stories about a thin stranger who was always lurking about the Opera.

One night I heard a couple whispering. "That cannot be a man!" said the woman. "I think it is a ghost!"

"Yes!" said the man. "He must be the Phantom of the Opera!"

I laughed to myself. What fun! From that moment on I was the Opera Ghost—the Phantom of the Opera!

Imagine my delight! Even the managers—those smart business-men—feared me!

I bought a bottle of ink the color of blood and wrote to them:

> Dear Managers,
>   A ghost who loves music haunts your Opera House! I ask you to let me have Box Five each night.
>   Sincerely,
>   The Opera Ghost

The managers were afraid to say no. They did as I asked. Now I had my own box at the opera!

Getting the box had been easy.

What else could the Phantom of the Opera get?

I took out my red ink again. This time I asked for money. I told the managers to put it in an envelope and leave it in Box Five. Again they obeyed.

Now I was living! I heard all the great singers of Paris. The biggest star of all was Carlotta. Everyone thought her voice was wonderful. Carlotta thought so too!

I did not agree. Her high notes hurt my ears. But little did I dream then how I would change Carlotta's voice!

Chapter 6

One night, I went to the opera as usual. A young girl, Christine, had a small part. I listened as she sang. Her voice was beautiful, but sad. So sad. I knew the right teacher could make her voice perfect.

I could not stop thinking about Christine. One night I hid behind the wall of her dressing room. Throwing my voice into the room, I began to sing.

I peeked through a hole in the wall and saw her smile.

"Beautiful voice!" she called.

"Where are you?"

"With you!" I answered. "I heard you sing. Your voice is lovely. But your heart is sad."

She nodded. "It is true."

"Why are you sad?" I asked.

"My mother died when I was six," she told me. "My father and I went from fair to fair. Papa played the violin and taught me to sing. One day a man heard us. He brought us to Paris to play and sing here. Then my father became very ill." Tears filled her eyes.

"I am sorry," I told her.

"Before Father died," said Christine, "he told me about the Angel of Music. Papa said that the Angel visits all great musicians. He said he would send the Angel of Music to me from heaven. He has kept his promise."

Christine wiped her tears. "Oh, Voice!" she cried. "Is it you? Are you the Angel of Music?"

For a minute, I said nothing. Then I made up my mind. "Yes," I told her. "I am the Angel of Music!"

Christine wept with joy. "I am ready, Angel! Teach me to sing!"

And so I did. Each night after the performance, I went behind her dressing-room wall. I played the violin and we sang. How we sang!

Christine put her heart into her singing. Her voice was far better than Carlotta's.

But I warned her. "Sing this way only here with me!"

"Why, Voice?" she asked.

"Wait and see!" I said. "We will take all of Paris by surprise!"

Oh, how happy I was! I had told a little lie, yes. But I meant no harm.

Everything went well for three months. Then one night Christine sang a small part as usual. When she came to her dressing room, she was very excited. Her eyes shone.

"I saw Raoul tonight!" she told me. "He was here! He heard me sing!"

"Who is Raoul?" I asked.

I sensed danger.

"I knew him as a child." She blushed. "Now he is a man. And so handsome!"

A handsome young man made Christine's eyes shine! I could not speak. Fear of losing her froze my words.

"Voice!" she called to me. "Are you still there?"

I could not answer.

Yet the next night, I returned to my place behind the wall. Christine was in her dressing room.

"Christine," I said. "The Angel of Music is here."

"Oh, Voice!" she cried. "How happy I am that you came back. I missed you so!"

"Christine," I said, "do you love someone here on earth? If you do, I must return to heaven. I must go away forever."

"Go away?" Christine gasped. "Forever? Oh no, Voice! No!"

"Then you must love only me, Christine," I told her.

Christine was quiet. At last she said, "Raoul is no more than a brother to me—a friend."

Her words made me happy. I knew so little of love, I believed her. Our lessons went on as before. Christine was almost ready to sing for the people of Paris.

Chapter 7

One day the newspaper said the Opera House managers were leaving. There would be a big party for the new managers after the performance. Carlotta had the leading role. All the important people of Paris would come. All the great singers would be there.

I had other ideas. I got out my red ink.

Dear Carlotta,
You will not sing tonight. Say you are ill. Do not even *think* of coming to the Opera House.
Beware!
The Opera Ghost

Night fell. It was almost time for the curtain to go up. Carlotta was not at the Opera House.

"Quick!" the stage manager called to Christine. "Put on Carlotta's costume. You will have to sing her part!"

Christine sang like an angel! People rose from their seats and clapped. They shouted, "Bravo! Bravo!" Christine was a new star!

After the opera, I rushed to the wall behind her dressing room. Christine ran in. Then someone ran in after her—Raoul! He tried to take her hand. Christine begged him to leave. I was not sure she meant it.

"Christine," I said after he had gone. "You love him, don't you?"

Christine sobbed. "I love only the Angel of Music!"

How I wanted to believe her! At last I did.

After that night, things did not go well. My poor Christine! When Carlotta heard about her great success, she was jealous! She made sure Christine did not get any more good parts to sing.

Even worse, the new managers did not believe in the Opera Ghost. They did not give me my money! They dared to take Box Five for themselves!

Well, they could not get away with it. I got out my red ink.

Dear New Managers,
1. Give me back Box Five!
2. Give me my allowance! Put it in an envelope and leave it in Box Five.

3. Carlotta will be ill tonight and Christine will sing in her place.

Disobey me, and I will curse this Opera House!

The Opera Ghost

I dipped my pen into the ink again.

Dear Carlotta,
You have a bad cold. If you sing tonight, you will be sorry. It will be worse than death!

The Opera Ghost

If my letters were not enough, the Opera Ghost had other tricks. Many tricks!

That night, I dressed for the opera and hid backstage. When no one was looking, I climbed up to the rafters. I worked carefully.

When I had finished, I went to Box Five. But the new managers were sitting there—in *my* box!

Rushing backstage, I nearly bumped into Carlotta! So, she had not obeyed my letter either! Well, she would learn. They would all learn. The Opera Ghost would teach them a lesson!

Chapter 8

The opera began. Christine sang a small part. Then Carlotta came onstage. Everyone clapped. She waited until they stopped before she began.

"Oh, how strange!" she sang. *"Like a spell* . . . CROAK!"

Carlotta grabbed her throat! The audience gasped! Carlotta sounded like a bullfrog!

She tried again. *"I feel* . . . CROAK! *All my heart* . . . CROAK!"

I crept up a secret passage behind Box Five. I whispered to the managers. "Carlotta is singing tonight to

bring down the lights!"

The managers looked around. Who had spoken? Then they looked up. The huge chandelier that hung over the hall was swaying back and forth. Back and forth. Faster and faster. And then . . . Crash! It fell!

"A little present from the Opera Ghost!" I howled.

The audience screamed in terror. People jumped from their seats, confused and frightened. There were dead and wounded among them.

Meanwhile, Christine had fainted on the stage. I leaped to where she lay and carried her through a secret passage. I had left a white horse from the stable in the first cellar. I put

Christine on his back and I took her down, down, down.

When we reached the lake, I lifted Christine off and freed the horse. I put Christine into a boat and rowed her to my house.

I carried her inside and helped her into a chair. She began to wake up.

"Who . . . who are you?" she asked in horror.

"Don't be afraid, Christine," I said. "You are in no danger."

"The Voice!" she cried. "The Angel of Music is . . . is a man!"

In a helpless rage, she rushed toward me, striking out with her fists. Then she began to weep.

"No, I am not an angel," I told her. "I am only Erik, a man who would do anything for you." I fell on my knees. "I beg you to forgive me!"

"I can only hate you for tricking me!" she sobbed. "Let me go!"

"You are free to go," I said sadly. "I will show you the way back up, Christine. But first let me sing to you."

I sang my sweetest song. And as I sang, Christine fell asleep.

I carried her into the second bedroom. I had filled it with flowers for her.

The next morning before she awoke, I wrote her a note. It said I was going out to buy some things. Then I locked the door.

When I came back, I had wonderful gifts for Christine. Hats, scarves, gloves! She brushed them all away.

"Take off your mask!" she demanded. "A good man does not need a mask."

"You shall never see my face!" I told her. "Now get ready for lunch."

I left her room, turning to bow to her. Christine slammed the door in my face.

She was not so angry when she came out.

She sat across from me at my table.

"I love you, Christine," I said. "Stay here with me for a few days. You will learn not to notice my mask. You will learn to know me. Then you may go. But I hope you will come back to see your Erik from time to time."

We talked for a while. "May I show you my home?" I asked. I reached for her hand. Christine screamed! She drew her hand away.

"Oh!" she cried in disgust. "You feel like . . ."

"Like death?" I finished the thought for her.

Without meaning to, I moaned! For a few minutes, I had forgotten that I was Erik. Erik, the Living-Dead Boy! Erik, the Living Skeleton!

After that, I was careful not to

touch Christine again. When we both had calmed down, I showed her my house. In the middle of my bedroom was an open coffin. "This is where I sleep," I said.

Christine turned her head away quickly and saw the beautiful organ. She walked over to it and picked up some sheets of my music.

"Are you writing an opera?" she asked.

"Yes," I said. "It is my great work. I began it many years ago. I work on it for two weeks at a time, never stopping to eat or sleep. Then I rest. Sometimes for months!"

"Will you play it for me?" she asked.

I shook my head. "It is not for your ears. It is filled with so much pain and so much love. Hearing it would break your tender heart."

I sat down at the organ and played other songs for her. Soon we were singing together. And then, in the middle of a song, Christine reached out. She ripped away my mask and screamed!

Chapter 9

Imagine my sorrow and rage as she stared at my death's head! At the two dark circles that ring my little yellow eyes! At the hole that serves as my nose! At my sunken mouth!

"So, you wanted to see?" I hissed. "Go ahead! Look at Erik's face! I am very handsome, am I not?"

I grabbed her hands and pressed them to my face. I made her nails dig into my skin! "You think this face is another mask? Try to tear it off!"

"Stop!" she cried. "Stop!"

"I am made of death!" I screamed.

"It is the Living Corpse who loves you! Now I must keep you here forever. Now that you have seen me, you would never come back!"

I pushed her into her room and flung myself into my music. My opera—the only thing I had left! I played, not caring if she heard.

After a while, Christine came out of her room. "Erik," she said. "Your face does not matter. I hear in your music how unhappy you are. But I also hear your great gifts. This music is more wonderful than any music I could imagine. In your own way, you *are* the Angel of Music!"

Were my ears playing tricks? Could she talk to me this way after she had seen my face?

I ran to her and kissed the hem of her dress. At last! Someone knew me for myself and did not scream or run away!

Christine stayed with me of her own free will. She threw my mask into the fire. With her, I could be myself! I trusted her.

We did not stay underground all the time. No! We went for carriage rides like other men and women. Once, I saw *him*. Raoul! He called to Christine, but she did not seem to hear him.

One afternoon Christine pointed to a locked door in her room. "Where does this door go?" she asked. "I have never seen you open it."

"You must never open it either," I said.

"Why?" she asked.

"It leads to a strange torture chamber I invented," I said. "I have enemies. I may need to use it someday." I smiled at Christine. "Now, let us talk of other things. Better yet, let us sing!"

We sang like two angels in heaven. Yet we were far, far underground.

A few days later, I was in the first cellar. Suddenly I felt a hand on my shoulder—it belonged to the Persian.

"A young singer is missing," he said. "Her name is Christine. Do you know where she is?"

"She is in my house," I said.

"You must let her go!" said the Persian.

"She is not my prisoner," I answered. "She wants to be with me."

I saw that the Persian did not

believe me. Not at all.

"It is true!" I cried. "She loves me. Yes, me! Erik! I am loved for myself! And I can prove it!"

"How?" asked the Persian.

"We are going to a masked ball tomorrow night," I said. "It will be in the grand hall of the Opera House. You must go too. When it is over, Christine will come home with me. She will come of her own free will."

The Persian nodded and walked away.

The next night we dressed for the ball. Christine wore a black cloak with a hood and a little black mask. No one would guess she was the missing singer. As for myself, I wore red. All red. I went as Red Death. And I had the perfect mask—no mask at all!

The Persian was there when we arrived. He saw that I let Christine go off. She talked with a man dressed in white. Was Raoul behind the mask?

After the ball, Christine went to her dressing room. Since her door was open, the Persian could see her. From behind the wall, I sang to Christine.

The Persian heard her say, "I am ready, Erik! Let us go home." I knew he would bother me no more.

Then, who should rush into her dressing room? The man in white—Raoul!

"Christine!" he called.

But he was too late. Christine was in my power. The power of my voice! I stood behind the mirror. Christine stood in front of it. "I am ready," she said.

Christine seemed to fade into the trick mirror. She was carried behind the wall to me. Raoul was left alone in her dressing room. Alone and confused, wondering where Christine had gone! How could that handsome young man guess she had gone to meet the Opera Ghost!

Chapter 10

Yes, Christine came back to me. I loved her with all my heart. And I was sure that she loved me.

When Christine had been with me two weeks, she felt it was time for her to go. Before she left, I slipped a gold ring on her finger. "Wear this ring always and think of your Erik. Do not lose it, Christine. If you do, beware!"

Christine looked at the ring. She shuddered a little bit as I led her up to her dressing room.

"I will come back to you, Erik," Christine said. "You have my word."

I was so full of love. "One more thing," I said. "This Raoul—I know he loves you. In a month, he is leaving Paris to explore the North Pole."

Christine nodded. "I know," she said.

"You have made me so happy, Christine," I told her. "You can make him just as happy. Go ahead. Spend time with him this month. I trust you, Christine, because I know you love me! Just promise to visit me."

Christine smiled at me. Her eyes shone. "Yes!" she said. "I will! I will make him happy too!"

And then I let her go.

That night, Christine sang. What an opera! What a night! Everyone in the audience fell in love with Christine!

I felt a little bit jealous. Taking a

secret passage, I made my way to Raoul's box. I whispered, "See the ring Christine is wearing? You did not give it to her!"

"Who speaks to me?" Raoul asked. His eyes searched for the owner of the voice. I just laughed and disappeared.

Christine kept her word. She left Raoul to visit me many times. How I looked forward to seeing her. What music we made together! Then she would go back up to her world. Even so, Christine was never far out of my sight. I could not keep myself from following her.

On one visit, Christine picked up a sheet of music. The notes had been written. Crossed out. Written again. "How is your opera coming?" she asked in her sweet voice.

"It is almost finished," I said. I looked over her shoulder. I hummed the last few notes. "When you leave today, I will work on it."

But when she left, I could not work. All I could think of was Christine. So I left my house and followed her like a shadow.

I watched Christine meet Raoul outside her dressing room. "I must speak to you!" she said to him. "Come! Let us go to the rooftop!"

The rooftop? Why, I wondered?

Raoul followed her. And I followed them. Through endless doors and narrow passages. Up ladders. Across bridges. I was at their heels, but they never saw me. At last they came out on the roof and sat down.

"Why must we talk here?" asked Raoul.

"Erik never comes up here," she said. "Besides, he's working on his opera. We are safe."

Safe? What did my Christine mean? Was she not *safe* with Erik?

Then she turned to Raoul. "You must take me away!" she cried.

"Yes!" he answered. "That is my dearest wish. I will forget about the North Pole. We will go away together!" He reached out and took her

hands. "But what about Erik? You always want to go to him."

Christine shook her head. "Never completely," she said. "Erik is a sort of angel. A sad, dark angel. His music seems to cast a spell on me. And I go because I cannot bear to hurt him. Yet I am also afraid of him!"

Raoul looked at Christine. "I will take you away. We shall be married. I shall come for you tonight."

"Not tonight," said Christine. "I will sing for Erik one more time. Tomorrow night is soon enough."

Oh! My heart was breaking! I had been so sure Christine loved me! I could not hold back a cry of pain!

"What was that?" cried Raoul. "Was it Erik?"

"It could not be!" said Christine.

"He . . . he said he would be working!" She stood up and took Raoul's hand. "Hurry!" she said.

As they ran, the ring fell from Christine's finger. I picked it up.

"Now you have lost the ring, Christine!" I whispered. "Beware! Beware!"

Chapter 11

Tears ran down my cheeks as I climbed from the roof. Bitter tears. Christine did not love me. Worse— she pitied me! Feared me!

I ran to my organ. In a fit of madness, I finished my opera.

I knew what I had to do next. I made some sleeping powder. I crept all the way up to where a crew of men would work the opera lights. I put the powder into their tea.

Then I made sure the path to my house was very slippery. In the dark, it would be easy to slide off the path into my torture chamber!

That night, a huge crowd came to the Opera House. The lights were lowered. The curtain went up. Christine looked pale as she started to sing in a shaky voice.

Raoul stood in his box. Christine looked up at him. Then she began to sing her heart out. She sang in a heavenly voice. She was singing for him alone. Not for me!

Now was the time! I crept to the main light box. The man in charge of it was snoring. Good! I turned off the lights—all of them! The Paris Opera House was dark! Before anyone could do anything, the lights came back on. The stage looked the same. Except for one thing. Christine was gone!

People rushed to where she had stood. They ran behind the stage, calling, "Christine! Christine!" She did not answer. She could not answer. She was with me!

This time, she did not want to come to my house. I had to give her some sleeping powder too.

When she woke up in her room, I was standing over her.

"It is up to you, Christine," I said. "Shall I play the Wedding March or the Funeral March?"

"I . . . I do not understand," she said.

"Is it so hard?" I asked. "My great opera is finished. I can't go on living like this. Under the ground like a mole! I want a wife like everyone else! I want to take her out on Sundays! Marry me, Christine!"

She groaned.

"With a new mask," I said, "I can look like anybody else. No one will

stare at us. You will be happy. Day and night, we will sing!"

Christine was crying.

"There is no need to be afraid of me," I said. "Am I such a monster? All I want is to be loved for myself. You can make me gentle as a lamb."

Christine only shook her head and wept.

"You decide!" I told her. "Look at these two little boxes. In this one is a grasshopper. In this one, a scorpion."

I held the boxes before her. "If your answer is yes, press the scorpion. How happy we will be!" I smiled. Then my smile faded. "However, if your answer is no, press the grasshopper. How he will hop! Ka-bam! The whole

Opera House will hop with him!" I laughed a crazy laugh.

"What do you mean?" cried Christine.

"There is gunpowder beneath the floor. Enough for a small war! One push on the grasshopper can start it! You have until eleven tomorrow night to decide. We will die if you say no! And many others will die with us— buried under the Opera House forever!"

I tied her hands and left the house. I needed to be alone. How my poor heart ached! If only she would say yes. I knew I could make her happy! She would forget all about Raoul.

When I came back, Christine spoke to me gently. "Untie me, Erik," she said. "I am in pain."

"Of course, my love," I said. "I don't want to hurt you."

"Will you play for me?" she asked.

I sat down at the organ. Soon, I was lost in the music. Suddenly Christine's hand shot out and grabbed the keys that lay on the organ! Then she raced to her room. I ran after her. She was trying to unlock the door to the torture chamber!

I grabbed back my keys. "What do you think you are doing?"

Her smile didn't fool me. "Just playing," she said.

Then a low cry came from the torture chamber. Christine jumped.

"What was that?" I asked.

"I heard nothing!" Christine said quickly.

"I thought I heard a cry," I said.

"A cry?" said Christine. "Are you going mad, Erik? How could anyone get into this house?"

I didn't like the way she said that. She was shaking. Then I knew—she was lying!

"Aha!" I said. "I understand now! I have a guest in my torture chamber! Would you like to see?"

Chapter 12

I opened up the hidden window in the wall. I turned on the lights in the torture chamber.

"You look, Christine," I said.

She went to the window. "No one is there," she said, hoping to fool me. But I knew that Raoul would try to find her. I knew who was in my torture chamber!

"No one?" I asked.

"No one," she said. "And it only looks like a forest anyway."

"Yes, yes," I said. "A forest of mirrors and torture beyond anything you could imagine. But I am growing tired of it. I want a wife like everybody else!"

Christine could not stop looking through the window. The forest was now very bright. "Put out the lights," she said. "Please!"

"Why?" I asked. "If no one is there?"

Christine looked pale and worried.

"I will do some tricks," I said. "They will take your mind off our guest. Listen!"

I threw my voice. I threw my voice all over the room. Croak! I made a frog sing like Carlotta!

"The wall of my room is getting hot!" said Christine. "Please! Put out the lights! The wall is burning hot!"

"Yes!" I said angrily. "The lights make the forest hot enough to roast a person alive!"

Christine fainted.

"Erik! Erik!" I looked through the window and saw Raoul. And the Persian! Ha! It served both of them right!

"Help us!" they cried. "We are burning alive! Water! Please! Give us water!"

"I will give you water," I called back with a wild laugh.

I pressed a button. The sound of

rain came into the torture chamber. Raoul and the Persian crawled toward the sound. Their swollen tongues were hanging out. They bent to lap up the rain. Ha! There was no rain. None at all! Their fat tongues licked the burning mirror. Oh, how they screamed in pain!

The screams woke Christine. "Erik!" she cried. "The answer is yes! I will be your wife."

She pressed the scorpion box. We heard the sound of water rushing below us.

"What do I hear?" she asked me.

"It is a flood," I told her. "Water will soak the gunpowder. Now the Opera House is safe. I cannot blow it up."

The water rose into the torture chamber. Raoul and the Persian tried to swim. The water rose higher. There was no air left!

Christine turned to me. "I beg you to save them," she said. "I beg you . . . as your wife!"

I looked into her innocent blue eyes. Christine looked back at me.

"I will marry you, Erik," she said. "Only save them."

Yes, she was telling the truth. "I will do it," I told her. "For you, my wife."

Chapter 13

I pressed a button and the water stopped. I pulled Raoul and the Persian out of the torture chamber. I laid them on the floor to push the water out of them. At last they began to breathe again.

I called a carriage to take the Persian to his home. I locked Raoul in a dungeon. I did not know what I would do with him. Not yet.

Then I came back to Christine. She was waiting for me like a bride! I bent to kiss her forehead. She did not step back. I kissed her. It was the first time I had ever kissed a human in my life! Now I knew happiness. I wept for joy.

Christine took my hand. "Poor unhappy Erik!" she said.

My heart had been full of hate. I was a monster. I had been ready to blow up the Paris Opera House and everyone in it! Now a change took place inside me. All I could think of was giving real happiness to Christine.

"I want you to have this." I slipped the gold ring on Christine's finger again.

"Yes, Erik," said Christine. "I am yours forever."

I know she meant it. She would stay with me. And she would try to love me.

I shook my head. My heart was spilling over with love.

"The ring is for you. And for Raoul," I told her. "It is my wedding present to you both."

Christine shook her head. "I do not understand!"

"I know you love him, Christine," I said. "Do not cry anymore! You have shown me love. Real love!"

"Yes, Erik," said Christine, "I do love you."

"Because you have loved me," I went on, "I can let you go. You are free to marry Raoul."

Christine grabbed my hand. Tears ran down her sweet face.

I went to the dungeon and led Raoul back to Christine. They put their arms around each other and they kissed. That kiss was like a knife in my heart. I knew then that I was dying. Dying of love.

"Wear the ring always, Christine," I said.

"Always," she whispered.

"And promise me one thing," I said.

"Anything, Erik," she said.

"I will send word just before I die," I told her. "Come back and put the ring on my finger, Christine. And bury me in secret."

"Bury you?" Christine asked.

"Yes," I said. "For I am dying now. I know you will come."

Christine nodded. And then she took my head in her hands. She drew me to her and kissed my forehead. A kiss! Given of her own free will!

Then I watched Christine and Raoul leave my house. Up, up they went into the world of the living. This time, I did not follow them.

Weeks have passed. Christine and Raoul have gone away together. They have gone to the northern country where Christine lived when she was a girl. She will come back when she hears from me. I know she will.

It will not be long now. I have known so little love. How strange that I am dying of it. I know more of death

than of life anyway.

Did I live? Not much. Oh, I could have written such music! Music that would live forever! Instead, I have burned my opera. No one shall ever listen to its magical notes.

Here in my home under the Paris Opera House, I shall die. Erik, the Living-Dead Boy. Erik, the Living Skeleton. Erik—the Phantom of the Opera.

Kate McMullan is not an opera fan. But she has been interested in special effects and in ghosts for many years. She also wrote the adaptation of *Dr. Jekyll and Mr. Hyde* for the Stepping Stone Book Classics series. She and her husband live in New York City with their daughter, who loves scary stories.

Paul Jennis loves opera and everything about the theater—costumes, scenery, dramatic lighting. And like the Phantom of the Opera, he plays keyboard instruments. Unlike the Phantom, however, he also plays basketball and golf. His outside interests serve his work well. Mr. Jennis's work often appears in sports magazines. He lives in Matawan, New Jersey.